W9-BVG-805

Too Many
TAMALES

GARY SOTO

illustrated by ED MARTINEZ

G. P. Putnam's Sons   New York

To Nancy Mellor
—G.S.

To my best friend, my wife, Debbi
—E.M.

Text copyright ©1993 by Gary Soto

Illustrations copyright ©1993 by Ed Martinez

All rights reserved. This book, or parts thereof, may not be reproduced

in any form without permission in writing from the publisher.

G. P. Putnam's Sons, a division of The Putnam & Grosset Group,

200 Madison Avenue, New York, NY 10016. Published simultaneously in Canada.

Printed in Hong Kong by South China Printing Co. (1988) Ltd.

Book design by Patrick Collins

The text is set in Berkeley Oldstyle

Library of Congress Cataloging-in-Publication Data

Soto, Gary. Too many tamales / by Gary Soto;

illustrated by Ed Martinez. p. cm.

Summary: Maria tries on her mother's wedding ring while helping

make tamales for a Christmas family get-together. Panic ensues

when, hours later, she realizes the ring is missing.

[1. Christmas—Fiction. 2. Mexican Americans—Fiction.

3. Rings—Fiction.] I. Martinez, Ed, ill. II. Title.

PZ7.S7242To 1993 [E]—dc20

91-19229 CIP AC

ISBN 0-399-22146-8

13 15 17 19 20 18 16 14

PaperStar edition 0-698-11412-4 (English)

PaperStar edition 0-698-11413-2 (Spanish)

Snow drifted through the streets and now that it was dusk, Christmas trees glittered in the windows.

Maria moved her nose off the glass and came back to the counter. She was acting grown-up now, helping her mother make tamales. Their hands were sticky with *masa*.

"That's very good," her mother said.

Maria happily kneaded the *masa*. She felt grown-up, wearing her mother's apron. Her mom had even let her wear lipstick and perfume. If only I could wear Mom's ring, she thought to herself.

Maria's mother had placed her diamond ring on the kitchen counter. Maria loved that ring. She loved how it sparkled, like their Christmas tree lights.

When her mother left the kitchen to answer the telephone, Maria couldn't help herself. She wiped her hands on the apron and looked back at the door.

"I'll wear the ring for just a minute," she said to herself.

The ring sparkled on her thumb.

Maria returned to kneading the *masa*, her hands pumping up and down. On her thumb the ring disappeared, then reappeared in the sticky glob of dough.

Her mother returned and took the bowl from her. "Go get your father for this part," she said.

Then the three of them began to spread *masa* onto corn husks. Maria's father helped by plopping a spoonful of meat in the center and folding the husk. He then placed them in a large pot on the stove.

They made twenty-four tamales as the windows grew white with delicious-smelling curls of steam.

A few hours later the family came over with armfuls of bright presents: her grandparents, her uncle and aunt, and her cousins Dolores, Teresa, and Danny.

Maria kissed everyone hello. Then she grabbed Dolores by the arm and took her upstairs to play, with the other cousins tagging along after them.

They cut out pictures from the newspaper, pictures of toys they were hoping were wrapped and sitting underneath the Christmas tree. As Maria was snipping out a picture of a pearl necklace, a shock spread through her body.

"The ring!" she screamed.
Everyone stared at her. "What ring?" Dolores asked.
Without answering, Maria ran to the kitchen.

The steaming tamales lay piled on a platter. The ring is inside one of the tamales, she thought to herself. It must have come off when I was kneading the *masa*.

Dolores, Teresa, and Danny skidded into the kitchen behind her.

"Help me!" Maria cried.

They looked at each other. Danny piped up first. "What do you want us to do?"

"Eat them," she said. "If you bite something hard, tell me."

The four of them started eating. They ripped off the husks and bit into them. The first one was good, the second one pretty good, but by the third tamale, they were tired of the taste.

"Keep eating," Maria scolded.

Corn husks littered the floor. Their stomachs were stretched till they hurt, but the cousins kept eating until only one tamale remained on the plate.

"This must be it," she said. "The ring must be in that one! We'll each take a bite. You first, Danny."

Danny was the youngest, so he didn't argue. He took a bite. Nothing.

Dolores took a bite. Nothing. Teresa took a big bite. Still nothing. It was Maria's turn. She took a deep breath and slowly, gently, bit into the last mouthful of tamale.

Nothing!

"Didn't any of you bite something hard?" Maria asked.

Danny frowned. "I think I swallowed something hard," he said.

"Swallowed it!" Maria cried, her eyes big with worry. She looked inside his mouth.

Teresa said, "I didn't bite into anything hard, but I think I'm sick." She held her stomach with both hands. Maria didn't dare look into Teresa's mouth!

She wanted to throw herself onto the floor and cry. The ring was now in her cousin's throat, or worse, his belly. How in the world could she tell her mother?

But I have to, she thought.

She could feel tears pressing to get out as she walked into the living room where the grown-ups sat talking.

They chattered so loudly that Maria didn't know how to interrupt.
Finally she tugged on her mother's sleeve.

"What's the matter?" her mother asked. She took Maria's hand.

"I did something wrong," Maria sobbed.

"What?" her mother asked.

Maria thought about the beautiful ring that was now sitting inside Danny's belly, and got ready to confess.

Then she gasped. The ring was on her mother's finger, bright as ever.

"The ring!" Maria nearly screamed.

Maria's mother scraped off a flake of dried *masa*. "You were playing with it?" she said, smiling gently.

"I wanted to wear it," Maria said, looking down at the rug. Then she told them all about how they'd eaten the tamales.

Her mother moved the ring a little on her finger. It winked a silvery light. Maria looked up and Aunt Rosa winked at her, too.

"Well, it looks like we all have to cook up another batch of tamales," Rosa said cheerfully.

Maria held her full stomach as everyone filed into the kitchen, joking and laughing. At first she still felt like crying as she kneaded a great bowl of *masa*, next to Aunt Rosa. As she pumped her hands up and down, a leftover tear fell from her eyelashes into the bowl and for just a second rested on her finger, sparkling like a jewel.

Then Rosa nudged her with her elbow and said, "Hey, *niña*, it's not so bad. Everyone knows that the second batch of tamales always tastes better than the first, right?"

When Dolores, Teresa, and Danny heard that from the other side of the room they let off a groan the size of twenty-four tamales.

Then Maria couldn't help herself: She laughed. And pretty soon everyone else was laughing, including her mother. And when Maria put her hands back into the bowl of *masa*, the leftover tear was gone.

2 1982 01101 5520

URBANA

URBANA